JUDITH CASELEY

BULLY

Greenwillow Books
An Imprint of HarperCollinsPublishers

Special thanks to Mrs. Cavolo
for her "brave words"

Bully
Copyright © 2001 by Judith Caseley
All rights reserved.
Printed in Hong Kong by South China Printing Company (1988) Ltd.
www.harperchildrens.com

Watercolor paints, colored pencils, and a black pen
were used to prepare the full-color art.
The text type is Souvenir Medium.

Library of Congress Cataloging-in-Publication Data
Caseley, Judith.
Bully / by Judith Caseley.
p.   cm.
"Greenwillow Books."
Summary: Mickey has trouble with Jack, a bully at school,
until he decides to try being nice to Jack
and making him a friend.
ISBN 0-688-17867-7 (trade). ISBN 0-688-17868-5 (lib. bdg.)
[1. Bullies—Fiction. 2. Schools—Fiction.] I. Title.
PZ7.C2677 Bu 2001 [E]—dc21 00-034106

1 2 3 4 5 6 7 8 9 10

First Edition

FOR MY MOTHER,
WHOM I ADORE

Mickey and Longjohn met their
friends at the park. Troy and Ian were
playing catch. Jessica was climbing the monkey
bars. Jack was sliding headfirst down the slide.

"Watch me, watch me!" Jack called
to his mother.
"She didn't see you," Longjohn told
him. "She was changing the baby."
"Who cares," said Jack, and he
headed for the monkey bars.

"Watch me climb to the top!" he called.
"She didn't hear you," Mickey told him,
  climbing behind him. "The baby was crying."
"Who cares," said Jack, stepping hard on
  Mickey's hand.

"You're not my friend anymore!" said Mickey.

"Ask me if I care," said Jack.

"You used to be a mouse," said Mickey. "And now you've turned into a great big rat!"

Jack gave him a shove, saying, "Don't call me a rat!"

"I saw that," said his mother, and she took him home.

A few days later Mickey announced to his family, "I need more cookies in my lunch box, please."

"Three cookies is plenty," Mama said to Mickey.

"Plus a sandwich and an apple," Papa added.

"He throws the apple away," said Jenna, and Mickey glared at her.

"No more cookies," Mama said, and the subject was closed.

The next day at lunch in the school cafeteria, Mickey took
a peanut butter sandwich, three chocolate chip cookies,
a juice box, and a container of applesauce out of his lunch
box. He put his arms around his food as if he were making
a fort, and ate his lunch very carefully.

Jack reached over and grabbed the bag of cookies. "Tell
anybody and I'll deck you," he said.

Peanut butter stuck to the roof of Mickey's mouth. He wanted
his cookies back, but the words stuck in his throat, too.

"I'm glad I ate my cookies already," said Jessica.

"Maybe you should tell the teacher about Jack,"
said Longjohn.

"He's bigger than I am," Mickey answered.

♥ Dear Mickey—
Eat your
applesauce!
Don't throw it
away. Love,
Mom

$$\begin{array}{r} \overset{7}{\cancel{8}}\overset{}{6} \\ -\ 27 \\ \hline 59 \end{array} \qquad \begin{array}{r} 108 \\ -\ 32 \\ \hline 76 \end{array}$$

$\leftarrow \dfrac{1}{8}$

After lunch the children returned to their classrooms. Jack's seat stayed empty, which made Mickey happy. Maybe Jack had gotten sick from eating too many cookies. Maybe he was moving to another town. Or another state. Or country. Or planet.

Just as Mrs. Pringle began writing on the blackboard, Jack slid into his seat. He leaned toward Mickey, stuck his hand inside Mickey's desk, and found his pencil with the dinosaur eraser.

Then he broke it in half.

"That's for calling me a rat," he said, putting the pieces on Mickey's desk.

Read!
- Bring in permission slip.
- Do pages 36-38 in math book.

On Sunday Mickey helped Papa in the garden. "There's a bully at school, and his name is Jack," he told his father. "He used to be my friend, but now he eats my cookies and breaks my pencils in half."

"Maybe if you use your brave words . . . ," said Papa, putting the watering can down. "Practice saying, 'I don't like that!' or 'Stop! You're hurting me.'"

"I don't like that!" Mickey said loudly.

"That's right," said Papa. "Stand your ground. In my experience most bullies are cowards." Then he began to water the geraniums.

The next day Mickey hid his cookies in his pocket. As he walked down the aisle of the cafeteria, his lunch box in his hand, someone stuck a foot out in front of him. Down went Mickey, and up went the lunch box, snapping open in midair. His juice box went flying, and his sandwich followed, which Jessica stepped on by mistake. The applesauce container rolled a few tables back.

If he called for help, was he using his brave words? Mickey stared at Jack. He didn't look like a coward. Jack stared back at Mickey. Jack didn't act like one, either.

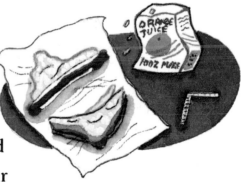

Mickey sat down as far away from Jack as he could possibly get. It was hard to stand your ground when your juice box was crushed and your sandwich was squished and your applesauce container was underneath another table.

"No, thanks," said Mickey when Jessica offered him a sandwich. He didn't like bologna, anyway.

On the weekend Mama took Mickey to see a movie about bugs.
The lights went down. They sat waiting in the dark.
"Do you remember Jack?" Mickey whispered to his mother.
"We used to be friends, and now he eats my cookies and
   he trips me in the lunchroom. If I were a bug, he'd squash me."
"Didn't Jack's mother have a baby?" Mama whispered. "Maybe
   that's why he's acting that way. Jack isn't the only child anymore.
   When you were born, your sister didn't like it. She wheeled
   you down the street and tried to give you to a neighbor."

"Really?" said Mickey.

"Really," said Mama. "Have you ever heard the saying, 'Love thine enemy'?"

"No," said Mickey. "What does it mean?"

"It means," said Mama, "that you might try being nice to him."

Mickey started to say, "He already gets to eat my cookies," but the movie had begun.

On Monday the class took a bus to the museum. Mickey sat beside Longjohn, and they played the alphabet game, using signs along the road. When they parked at the museum, they had only reached the letter C. There was a tap on Mickey's shoulder.

"C for Cap," said Jack, taking Mickey's baseball cap and tossing it across the aisle. Kyle caught the cap and threw it to Billy. Billy threw the hat as if it were a boomerang. It hit the teacher on the head.

"The owner of this has no recess tomorrow," said Mrs. Pringle. "And I keep the cap."

"It's hard to love your enemy," said Mickey to Longjohn.

"I couldn't do it," said Longjohn to Mickey.

Mickey and Jenna played ball that afternoon. Mickey dropped the ball for the fourteenth time. "The sun got in my eyes," he explained to Jenna.

"Where's your hat?" said Jenna, and Mickey told her about Jack.

"Mama says I should try being nice to him. Papa says that most bullies are cowards. I say Jack is ruining my day."

"Stick with Mama," Jenna said. "Bring him more cookies."

The next day at lunch Mickey pushed a bag of chocolate chip cookies down the long table until they got to Jack. Jack ate the cookies without saying a word.

Back in the classroom Mrs. Pringle returned the children's
homework. She handed Jack his paper, saying, "I liked
your story about your baby sister and your dog."
Everybody turned to look at Jack.
"It really happened," said Jack, smiling. And there were
brand-new braces on his big white teeth.

"Track mouth!" cried a voice from the back of the room.

"Track-mouth Jack!" said someone at the front.

"That's enough!" said Mrs. Pringle. "They look very nice. They're such a pretty blue."

Jack's face got red, and he scrunched down in his seat as if he were a turtle.

In the hallway after class Mickey said to Jack,
"Blue's my favorite color."

"Mine, too," said Jack in a very low voice.
"That's why I picked it."

"What's your story about?" asked Mickey.

"I made my baby sister laugh for the very first time
 since she was born."

"How?" said Mickey.

"I taught my dog to dance." Jack smiled once
 more, so that his blue braces flashed.

"When I was born," said Mickey, "my sister
 wanted to give me away to the neighbor."

"No kidding!" said Jack, and they started to laugh
 and didn't stop until a teacher shushed them.

At home after dinner Mickey asked Mama if he could play at Jack's the next day. "Jack's going to show me how he taught his dog to dance."

"Jack the bully? Were you nice to him?" said Mama.

"Did you use your brave words?" Papa asked.

"Did you bring him more cookies?" Jenna wanted to know.

"I tried everything," Mickey told them. "Then I made him laugh."

"Bully for you! I never thought of that," said Papa.

"Bully for you!" said Jenna and Mama.

"Bully for me!" said Mickey loudly, which made
the four of them laugh for the longest time.